Lauren's Little Free Library

*Dedicated to my family—
and to my family of friends!*

Henry Holt and Company, LLC
Publishers since 1866
175 Fifth Avenue, New York, New York 10010
mackids.com

Henry Holt® is a registered trademark of Henry Holt and Company, LLC.
Copyright © 2015 by Mike Curato
All rights reserved.

Library of Congress Cataloging-in-Publication Data
Curato, Mike, author, illustrator.
Little Elliot, big family / story and pictures by Mike Curato. — First edition.
pages   cm
Summary: At Mouse's house, Elliot the elephant finds more than a friend—he finds a family.
ISBN 978-0-8050-9826-6 (hardcover)
[1. Families—Fiction. 2. Friendship—Fiction. 3. Elephants—Fiction. 4. Mice—Fiction.] I. Title.
PZ7.C91757Lk 2015   [E]—dc23   2014044996

Henry Holt books may be purchased for business or promotional use. For information
on bulk purchases, please contact the Macmillan Corporate and Premium Sales Department
at (800) 221-7945 x5442 or by e-mail at specialmarkets@macmillan.com.

First edition—2015
The artist used pencil on paper and digital color in Adobe Photoshop to create the illustrations for this book.
Printed in China by RR Donnelley Asia Printing Solutions Ltd., Dongguan City, Guangdong Province

1   3   5   7   9   10   8   6   4   2

Little Elliot

Big Family

Story and pictures by

Mike Curato

Henry Holt and Company · New York

*L*ittle Elliot woke up
to a bright winter day.

"Good morning, Mouse!" said Elliot.

"Morning, Elliot," said Mouse.

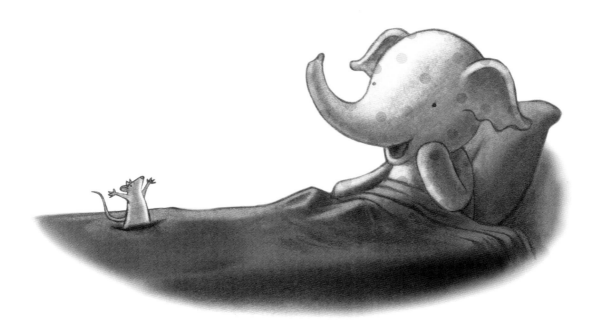

"Today is my family reunion. I can't wait for my grandmother's cheese chowder!

"I hope Grandmother made an extra-large batch. I have to share it with my parents, grandparents, 15 brothers, 19 sisters, 25 aunts, 27 uncles, and 147 cousins."

Mouse thought for a moment. "At least, I think that's right. It's very hard to keep track.

"I'd better go," said Mouse.
"I don't want to be late!"

"Have a good time!" said Elliot,
and with a wave, Mouse was off.

The house was quiet. And empty.

Elliot decided to take a walk.

He saw many families.

Brothers played in the street.

Mothers read to their sons.

Fathers took their daughters to the park.

Sisters shared treats (and secrets).

Grandmothers sang to babies
while uncles gave advice.

Cousins skated together.
Some even did tricks!

Elliot wondered what it would be like
to have 147 cousins. Or even just one.

It was getting cold, so Elliot
decided to see a movie.

The theater was big and dark.
And empty.

Elliot missed Mouse.

When Elliot left the theater, he discovered
that everything was blanketed in white.

The snow fell and the wind blew.

Elliot could hear his name. Was it the wind?

No, it was Mouse.

"I missed you!" said Mouse.

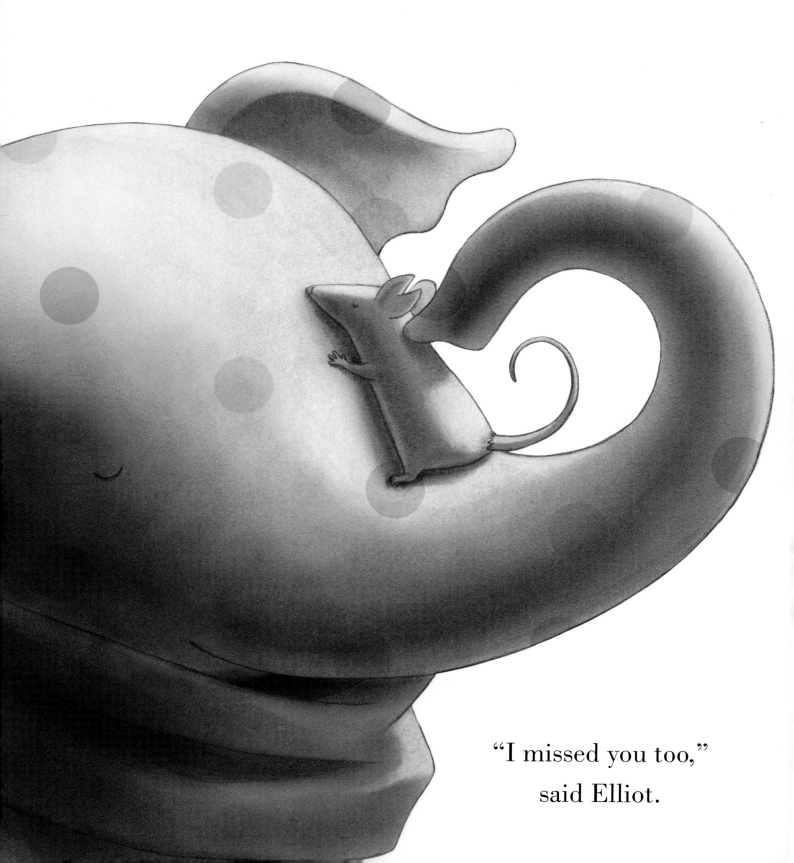

"I missed you too,"
said Elliot.

"Let's get out of the cold," said Mouse.
"I know somewhere we can go."

Mouse's family gave Elliot a warm welcome.
"Come, have some cheese chowder!"
said Mouse's grandmother.

The party went on for hours.

Elliot had a wonderful time!

At the end of
the day, Mouse
counted the whole
family again . . .

. . . and added one more.